JINX
AND THE
DOOM
FIGHT CRIME!

Story by
Lisa Mantchev

Pictures by
Samantha Cotterill

A Paula Wiseman Book
Simon & Schuster Books for Young Readers
New York London Toronto Sydney New Delhi

SIMON & SCHUSTER BOOKS FOR YOUNG READERS
An imprint of Simon & Schuster Children's Publishing Division
1230 Avenue of the Americas, New York, New York 10020
Text copyright © 2018 by Lisa Mantchev
Illustrations copyright © 2018 by Samantha Cotterill
SIMON & SCHUSTER BOOKS FOR YOUNG READERS is a trademark of Simon & Schuster, Inc.
For information about special discounts for bulk purchases, please contact Simon & Schuster
Special Sales at 1-866-506-1949 or business@simonandschuster.com.
The Simon & Schuster Speakers Bureau can bring authors to your live event.
For more information or to book an event, contact the Simon & Schuster Speakers Bureau
at 1-866-248-3049 or visit our website at www.simonspeakers.com.
Book design by Lizzy Bromley
The text for this book was set in Nouveau Crayon.
The illustrations for this book are hand drawn, paper cut, and digitally colored,
then set in a 3-D environment and photographed.
Manufactured in China
1117 SCP
First Edition
2 4 6 8 10 9 7 5 3 1
CIP data for this book is available from the Library of Congress.
ISBN 978-1-4814-6701-8
ISBN 978-1-4814-6702-5 (eBook)

This is Jinx.

This is her little brother, the Doom.

And together,

they FIGHT CRIME.

Well, first they get up,

have breakfast,

and brush their teeth . . .

but then they FIGHT CRIME!

They used to fight each other.

But then they realized they could use their powers for GOOD and not EVIL.

So now, they defend the innocent!

They protect the planet!

They stop to have lunch . . .

but then they get right

to FIGHTING CRIME!

Sometimes missions come from headquarters.

(Missions can get complicated.)

But when you FIGHT CRIME, you never give up.

When you FIGHT CRIME, you finish the job.

When you
FIGHT CRIME,
you make sure the
team stands strong.

And when you
FIGHT CRIME,
you help out
the little guy.

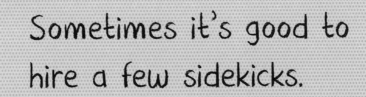

Sometimes it's good to
hire a few sidekicks.

The last thing before bed, Jinx and the Doom turn on the superhero signal to let the city know it's safe.

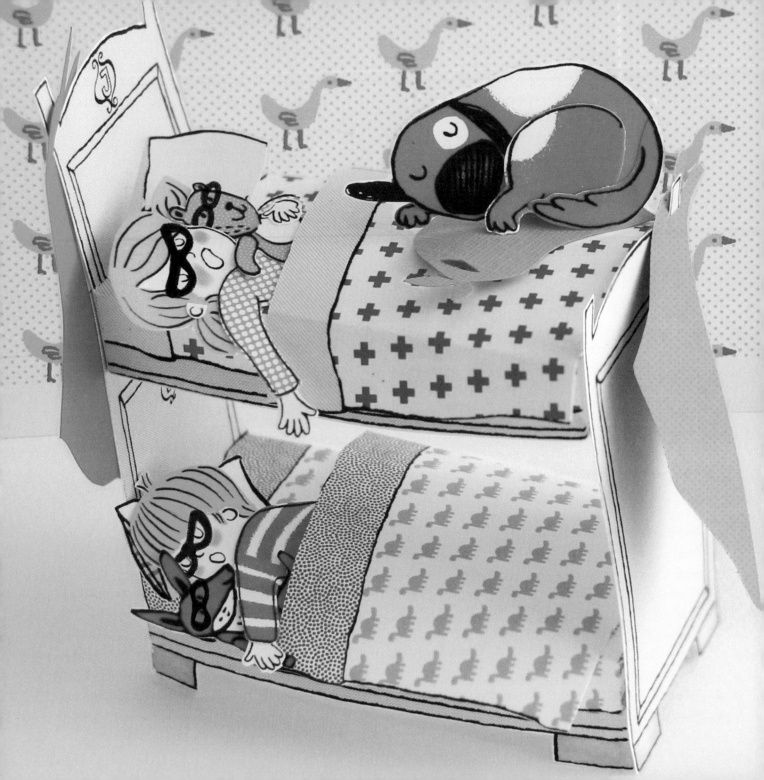

And then they get a good night's sleep, because tomorrow . . .

THEY WILL **FIGHT MORE CRIME!**